NO, I WON'T

MANICA K. MUSIL

WINDMILL BOOKS

Published in 2021 by Windmill Books, an Imprint of Rosen Publishing
29 East 21st Street, New York, NY 10010

Cataloging-in-Publication Data

Names: Musil, Manica K.
Title: No I won't / Manica K. Musil.
Description: New York : Windmill Books, 2021.
Identifiers: ISBN 9781499486612 (pbk.) | ISBN 9781499486629 (library bound) |
ISBN 9781499486865 (6 pack) | ISBN 9781499486636 (ebook)
Subjects: LCSH: Families–Juvenile fiction. | Obstinacy–Juvenile fiction. | Crocodiles–
Juvenile fiction.
Classification: LCC PZ7.1.M97.5 No 2021 | DDC [E]–dc23

Manufactured in the United States of America.

CPSIA Compliance Information: Batch #BS2OWM. For Further Information contact Rosen Publishing, New York, New York at 1-800-237-9932.

Find us on

4

My name's Karl. I have
a brother, a sister, and a mommy
who can be so annoying.

Brush
your teeth!

We already have.
Except for Karl.

Mine are
the whitest!

I don't want to
brush my teeth!

6

7

Whenever Mommy makes lunch, we have to eat every last bite.

I don't like soup!

Whenever we **play,** we all have **to clean up.**

Let's make some more mess!

Where are we off to?

In the evening, right when we're having lots of fun, Mommy usually says, "Get to bed—it's late!"

No, I still want to play!

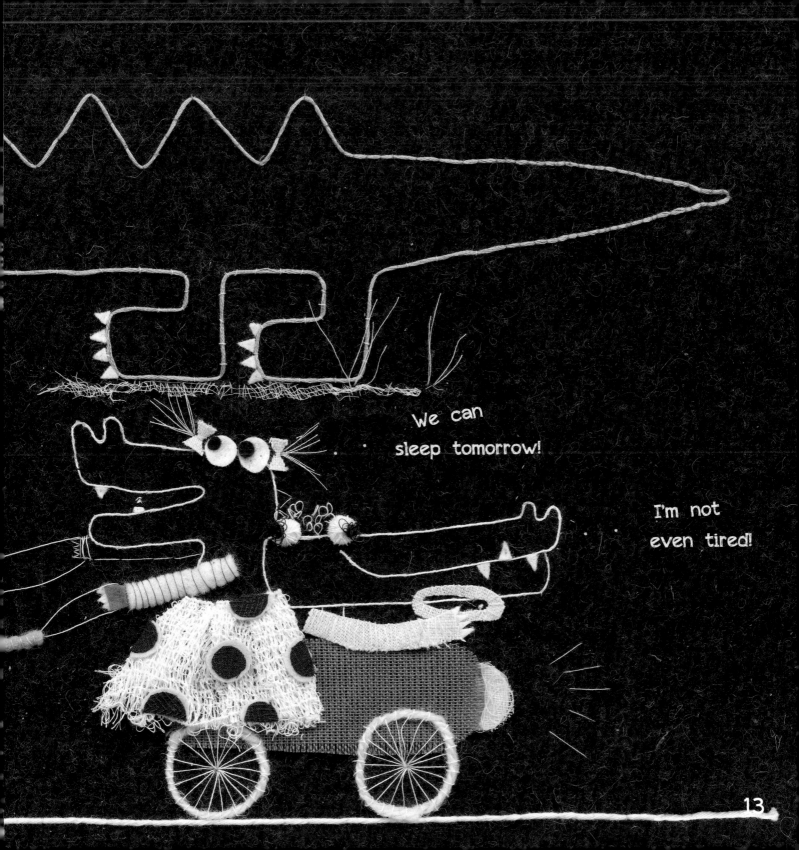

13

One day, I **decided** **not** **to** **listen** **anymore.**

Why do we have to listen to our parents?

14

Because they're both so smart!

So that we can get what we want!

15

Mommy asked me to help my sister with her homework. "No, I won't!" I said.

This homework is really tough!

When I was in first grade, I knew the answers to everything!

17

When a **rhinoceros** came to visit, Mommy said,
"Say hello, Karl!" "I don't want to!" I yelled.

What misbehaved children!

And yours always
listen to you?

Grrrr!

I sulked and moaned and whenever I heard my name, I said, "I don't want to!"

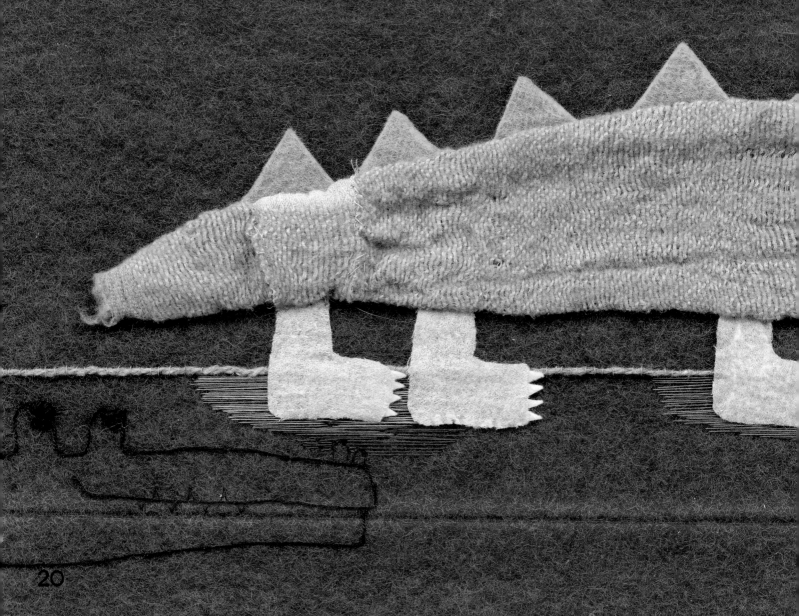

I'm never going
to listen again!

21

After a while, I started to feel guilty.
Great big tears came streaming out of my eyes.

Being alone
is so boooooooring!

Mommy was calm and said,

"Come here, let's make dinner together!"

where's my plate?
I want my plate!

That one's mine!

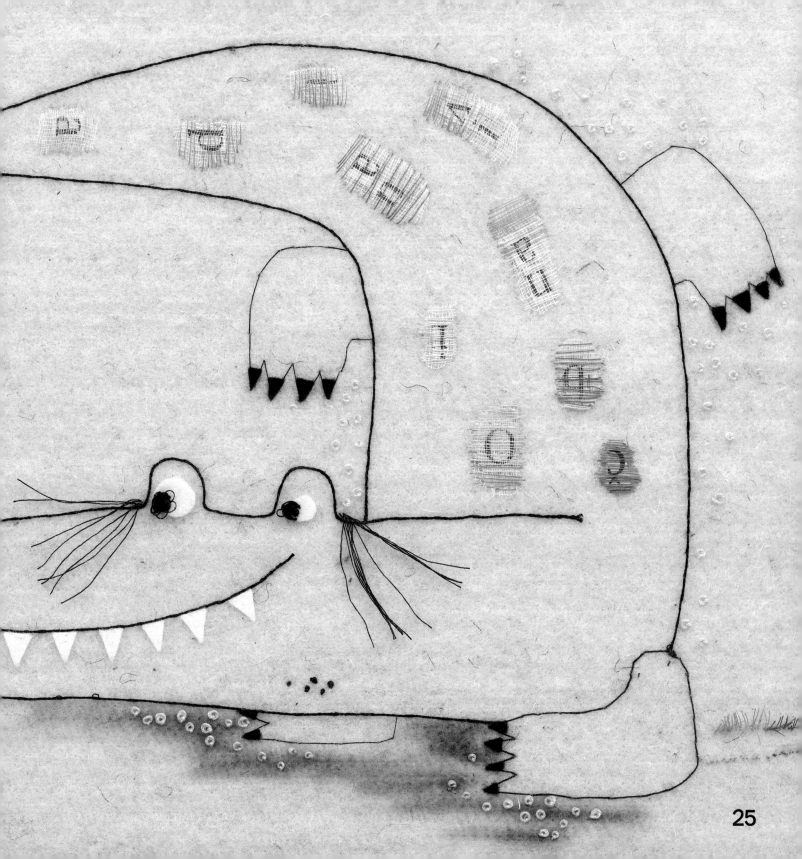

After dinner, we **fell asleep.**
I was very tired.

Where's Mommy?
I want a story!

I can tell
you one...

I don't want
a girl's story!

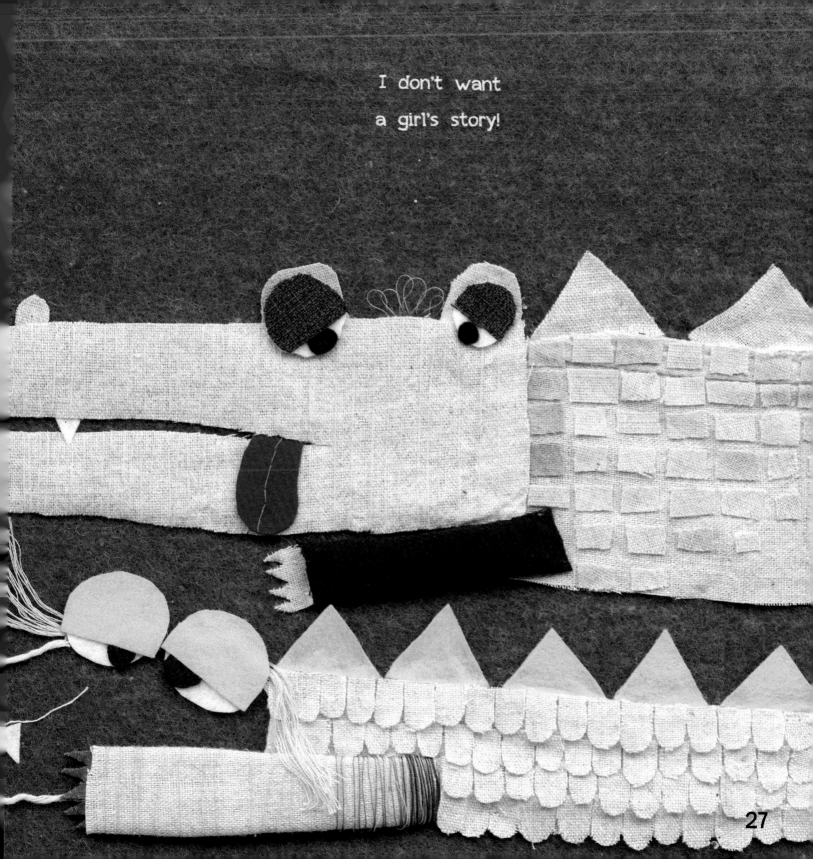

The next day Mommy said, "What a beautiful day! Why don't we take a little trip?" "No, I won't!" I said. It just slipped out – we all love to take trips. Everyone laughed.

29

Where are
we going?